Puffi ... mpanies
w ... .com.
... ɔ.uk

| UK

First published 2021

001

Text and illustrations copyright © Jion Sheibani, 2021

The moral right of the author/illustrator has been asserted

Text design by Mandy Norman
Printed and bound in China by RR Donnelley Asia Printing Solution Limited

A CIP catalogue record for this book is available from the British Library

ISBN: 978–0–241–43863–3

All correspondence to:
Puffin Books
Penguin Random House Children's
One Embassy Gardens, 8 Viaduct Gardens
London, SW11 7BW

MIX
Paper from
responsible sources
FSC® C018179
www.fsc.org

Penguin Random House is committed to a
sustainable future for our business, our readers
and our planet. This book is made from Forest
Stewardship Council® certified paper.

THE WORRIES

JAZ AND THE NEW BABY

Written and illustrated by
JION SHEIBANI

PUFFIN

Chapter 1

Jaz was **SO** excited. Any day now, she would be getting a baby sister. She'd been wanting one for such a long time. For weeks, she'd been helping Mum and Dad prepare.

Jaz didn't even mind that she had to change bedrooms. Dad had promised they would decorate her new room together, as soon as he finished the baby's room. It was going to be **BRILLIANT**. And so would being a big sister.

Jaz was a bit worried about one thing, though. It was nearly her birthday, and the baby was due just two days before.

Babies often came late, Mum said. What if she was born **ON** Jaz's birthday? Jaz had a really special party planned.

She'd been writing her party list for *months*! Besides, she didn't want to *share* her birthday with someone else **FOREVER**.

'Wouldn't that be funny?' said Mum.

'A real coincidence!' said Dad.

A real pain in the bum, thought Jaz.

It would be like being a twin, only without all the fun stuff of being a twin. Or having your birthday on Christmas Day, without all the fun stuff of Christmas Day.

But in the end, the baby came early. Two weeks early. Mum and Dad were in a right panic, especially Dad. Then Gran came round to look after Jaz and they watched her parents drive off to the hospital.

The flat felt very strange without them. So did her new bedroom, which wasn't even finished.

As Jaz tried to fall asleep that night,

she heard a familiar sound. It was the soft strumming of a guitar. Loner's guitar.

Loner was one of Jaz's Worries. He had first appeared when Jaz started her new school. He had been small to start with but **grew** and grew until it became very difficult to hide him.

Mum found him in the end, hidden in the bath. Together, Mum and Jaz had talked about ways to keep him small, like making friends, or playing music. Over time, Loner got smaller or fell asleep or even disappeared completely, like the time he went on holiday with her friend Sohal's Worries.

'Hey, dude,' she said, pulling Loner out

from under her bed by the ankle. 'What are you *doing*?'

'Whaddya mean, what are you doin'?' Loner moaned. 'I'm playing a **SAD** tune, which *you're* interrupting.'

'But, Loner, I'm fine! Why are
you **HERE**?'

'Of course you're not *fine*, man! Your
parents are at the hospital. You're
about to have a baby sis. You're feeling

L-O-N-E-L-Y!

That spells *lonely*, by the way. Now, if
you don't mind, I was in the middle of
composing a really cool song.'

Loner picked up his guitar and began to
sing again.

'Please stop,' Jaz said, covering her ears.
'You sound like a cat choking on a fur ball!'

'It's called the *blues*!' Loner grumbled.

'Well, can you play something *not* blue, dude?' said Jaz. 'You're making me even sadder. And I need to **sleep**!'

But Loner carried on with his tune. Like most Worries, he was pretty stubborn and did not like being told what to do.

Jaz got up and sneaked into the living room where Gran was snoring away on the sofa-bed. Jaz slipped under the quilt and **snuggled** up next to her. Gran's warm vanilla smell immediately made her feel better (and Gran's

snoring drowned out Loner's annoying music). As Jaz drifted off to sleep, she felt excited again.

By tomorrow, she thought,

MY LITTLE SISTER WILL BE HERE!

Chapter 2

The next morning, just as Jaz
was finishing her breakfast,
Gran's phone rang.

'THE BABY'S BORN!'

She grinned. 'Her name is Rosana. After
your great-great-great-
great-aunt! Isn't that
wonderful?'

Jaz did **NOT** think Rosana was a wonderful name. She'd definitely be calling her Roz. But it *was* cool that her sister was *finally* born.

'Can we go and see them now?' Jaz asked excitedly.

'They've got to do a few tests first.' Gran looked a bit serious. 'She had trouble breathing to begin with. And your mum is very tired. But don't worry, poppet, everything will be OK!'

Gran's phone **PINGED** and baby Roz's photo appeared. She was wrapped tightly in a blanket and had a tube up her nose.

'Oh, isn't she *gorgeous*?' Gran sighed. 'She's got your eyes!'

But Jaz found it hard to concentrate on Roz's face. All she could think about was the tube coming out of her nose and Gran's words, *She had trouble breathing . . . your mum is very tired . . .*

'When can we go and see her, then?' asked Jaz sulkily.

'Soon,' Gran said.

Ugh, SOON.

Jaz hated that word. Grown-ups were always using it. It basically meant, *I've absolutely no idea and please don't ask me any more questions.*

Jaz went out into the garden to play with her skateboard. She tried to have fun, but she had this strange feeling in her tummy.

She decided to go to her bedroom to add things to her party list. But just as she was writing the words GIANT UNICORN BALLOON, there came a

terrible RACKET

from her cupboard.

Oh no, not Loner again! thought Jaz.

She flung open the cupboard door and, sure enough, there was Loner. But another, furry, creature was there too, wearing big sunglasses, headphones and a baseball cap back to front. He was standing behind some DJ decks and *very* loud speakers.

'YO, YO, YO!'

he shouted into a microphone.
'It's **DJ Disaster!** The maddest,
baddest Worry in town! Put your hands
in the air like you just don't care!'

Oh, great, thought Jaz. *Another Worry!*

So *that* was what the funny feeling in her tummy was. Now she thought about it, she *was* worried about baby Roz. What was that tube for? Why couldn't Jaz visit her? Was she *really* going to be OK? Jaz hated not knowing.

DJ Disaster started playing the kind of music you might hear in a horror film. Loner was jumping up and down and **bobbing** his head excitedly.

'Hey,' Jaz shouted over the music.

'TURN IT DOWN!'

DJ Disaster couldn't hear, so Jaz turned to Loner instead. 'Hey, dude. What are you *doing*?'

'It's called head-banging!' Loner shouted. 'Cool music, huh?'

'It's even worse than your blue stuff.'

'It's called the BLUES!' Loner replied.

'Whatever, dude. Just get him to turn it down!'

'Oh, but he's my FRIEND, man!' moaned Loner. 'You're always telling me to make new friends. It keeps me small, you said.'

'Yes, I know but . . . maybe not friends called *Disaster*, OK? He's giving me a headache.'

Loner finally agreed to ask him to turn down the music.

'What a bunch of party poopers!' Disaster huffed. 'And I thought you were a **COOL** Worry.'

'I *am* a cool Worry!' Loner whined. '*Really* cool.'

Suddenly, there was a knock on Jaz's bedroom door.

'Everything OK, Jazzy?' Gran said softly. 'What's all that noise?!'

18

'Quick, hide!' Jaz whispered.

'No way, man!' Loner said, folding his arms. 'Remember what your mum said: never hide your Worries!'

'Well, Mum's not here,' Jaz said firmly. 'So you're gonna have to do what *I* say!'

Chapter 3

'**Good news!**' Gran said, when Jaz finally opened her door. 'We can go and visit Rosana this afternoon!'

Jaz was so relieved. She left Loner and Disaster in her cupboard while she changed into her favourite outfit. She decided to make Rosana a special card and a WELCOME HOME banner. Then she picked the first daffodils from the garden for Mum. By the time they left, Jaz had completely forgotten about her Worries. She was far too excited.

When they arrived at the hospital, Mum and Dad gave her an enormous hug. Mum was so happy to see Jaz, she even cried a little bit. Jaz always found it weird when adults did that. Crying meant being **SAD**, not happy! Feelings were already confusing enough without grown-ups mixing them up.

Mum reached into the cot beside her bed. She slowly lifted a small white bundle and cradled it in her arms.

'Meet your big sister!' Mum beamed.

Jaz sat down on the bed to get a better look. There she was! **Her SISTER!**

Jaz stared at Rosana's little pink face peeking out from under the crocheted hat Gran had made. The rest of her was buttoned up in soft white pyjamas and wrapped in Jaz's old baby blanket. She was even cuter than her photo. And the tube had gone.

'Would you like to hold her?' Mum asked.

Jaz thought how small and fragile Roz looked. She was worried she might break her or drop her. But Jaz didn't say that out loud. She just shook her head instead.

'That's OK,' Mum said, trying to hide her disappointment. 'Whenever you're ready, love!'

Jaz watched her parents and Gran cooing over baby Roz.

'Isn't she gorgeous!'

'Look at those tiny fingers!'

'Look at her little nose!'

After a while, Jaz realized that babies were actually **really** boring. Roz couldn't smile or talk or even gurgle. Jaz was starting to get hungry and impatient. She really needed to finish her party list. There was still so much to do: the invitations, the shopping, the decorations! She turned to Gran.

'Can we go home now?'

'We only just got here, Jazmin!' Gran sighed. 'You were in such a hurry to come, remember? It's not every day you get to meet your baby sister.'

'It's OK, the nurse will be here in a bit to check on Rosana,' said Mum. 'You two go home.'

'Are you coming, Dad?' Jaz asked hopefully.

'No, I'm staying another night to help out your mum. But all being well, we'll be home tomorrow. You be a good girl and make sure Rosana's room is ready, yeah?'

'Yeah,' Jaz mumbled. She wanted to say, *But what about decorating* my *bedroom? And what about* my *birthday party?* But she didn't, of course. She knew it would only make Dad frown and say something annoying like, 'Don't be *selfish*, Jazmin!'

Jaz didn't feel like it, but she hugged her Mum and Dad. She gave Roz a kiss on her forehead and was surprised by how good she smelled, like a warm, buttery croissant.

'Bye, dude,' she whispered.

Jaz turned round at the door to say goodbye, but her parents were cooing over Roz again and didn't look up.

It's OK, Jaz thought, as she shuffled down the corridor behind Gran.

I'm going to plan the **BEST BIRTHDAY PARTY** EVER.

Chapter 4

When Jaz got back to her bedroom, it looked like it had been burgled! It was **SUCH a mess**. She quickly shut the door so Gran couldn't see.

'LONER!' she hissed. 'I knew I shouldn't have left you in here! Just wait till I find you – and your little DJ mate.'

Jaz hunted high and low but Loner

and DJ Disaster were nowhere to be found. Suddenly, she heard the sound of **jangling** coins.

Jaz looked under her desk and found a small creature emptying her piggy bank on to the floor! The creature and the piggy bank were nearly the same size.

'Hey, LEAVE MY MONEY ALONE!'

Jaz shouted.

The creature looked up, but instead of looking scared it just smiled.

'Oh, hey there, sweetheart!' she said smoothly. 'I'm Jealousy! But you can call me Jel.'

'*Another* Worry?' Jaz groaned.

''Fraid so, honey. But I'm a lotta fun, you'll see!'

'So what do *you* worry about?'

'Not having **ENOUGH**, of course!'
Jel laughed dramatically.

'Enough of what?'

'Why, *everythin'*, honey! Love, mainly.
And money. Oh, and chocolate. I luuuuurve
chocolate.'

Jealousy started putting more coins from
the pile into a large handbag. She found a
pretty marble and popped that in there too.

'Put that BACK!' Jaz snapped.

'You've got some beeeautiful things here!'
Jel said, as if she hadn't heard. 'I helped
myself to a few – hope you don't mind!'

'So it was YOU who did this to my room?
What else have you got in there?'

Jaz picked up Jel's handbag and looked inside. 'OMG! That's my **ALIEN PET SHOP**™ club membership badge. You can't have that!'

'Oh, don't be such a tightwad!' Jel said, yanking the bag away from her. 'It was at the bottom of a drawer. You don't NEED it.'

'Well, neither do you!' Jaz yanked the bag back again.

'Listen, sweetie, I came here to help you,' Jel huffed.

'Oh, really?'

'Why, sure! I'm a professional party planner! And I heard it's your birthday soon.'

GREEN-EYED MONSTER
EVENTS

Contact Jealousy:
01234 567891
jealousy@greeneyedmonster.com

'Y'know, Jealousy throws the best parties in town!'

'OK . . .' said Jaz suspiciously. 'Well, I don't really need any help. I've already made a list. My mum and dad are gonna help me.'

'Are you *sure* about that, honey? They're pretty busy with your **GORGEOUS** li'l sister right now.'

'Well, yeah, but that's just for now.'

'If you say so!' Jel said mischievously. 'Well, don't hang around, sweetie. Show me this list already!'

Jaz opened her special sparkly notebook and reluctantly passed it to Jealousy.

'What? That's **IT?!**' Jel shrieked.

'What do you mean, that's *it*?'

'I mean, that AIN'T no party, *girl*!

It's pathetic, actually.'

Jel whipped a furry fluorescent pen
from her bag and started scribbling
all over the page.

'Isn't that *my* pen?' said Jaz.

'NO!' Jel gasped. 'How DARE
you!' She paused briefly. 'I took it
from one of your other Worries.
Whatshisname . . . Loser!'

'*Loner*,' Jaz corrected. 'Hey, what

are you writing anyway? Stop
crossing stuff out!'

Jaz looked over Jel's shoulder
and read. 'A magician?! A candy
floss machine?! A hot-dog *and* ice-
cream stand?! Mum and Dad will
NEVER agree to all this!'

'Well, it's my job to make them!'
Jel grinned wickedly. 'Just you see!'

Chapter 5

The next day, Mum, Dad and baby Roz were finally coming home. Jealousy was still asleep under Jaz's bed (she'd fallen asleep writing her **VERY** long list of Birthday-Party Demands). Jaz hoped she'd stay there for the rest of the day. She was very excited about her parents being home again. It was nice having Gran to stay, but it just wasn't the same.

Besides, Gran wasn't very interested in Jaz's party list. She kept saying things like:

In my day, we didn't have birthday parties.

We might have a cake, if we were lucky! My friend had a loaf of bread and one candle!

My only present was a hoop and stick. It was wonderful!

Children today are far too spoilt.

Handmade presents are best. I'll knit you another hat with your name on it.

'They're HERE!'

Jaz shouted.

She jumped down from the windowsill where she'd hung the WELCOME HOME banner and ran outside to the car.

It felt so good to hug Mum and Dad properly at last.

'What a lovely welcome!' said Mum.

'Thank you, love,' Dad said, looking at the banner. 'That's really nice.'

Jaz helped Dad bring her sister into the house in her carrycot. Today, Roz was wrapped up in a puffy blue all-in-one coat.

She looked like a very cute spacewoman.

Mum was still feeling pretty tired, so she sank on to the sofa straight away. Jaz squeezed some fresh orange juice for her and then arranged all the flowers and congratulations cards, including one that was attached to a balloon!

Jaz put her own card for Rosana on the mantelpiece, but it looked a bit lost among all the other big, sparkly ones. Just as Jaz was thinking this, Jealousy's head appeared from behind them.

'Hey, sweetie! You spoken to your folks about the party yet? We got a lot to do!'

'No! Go away,' Jaz whispered.

'They've only just got back!'

'Oh, go *on*, I know you're **DYING** to!'

'Hey, Jaz,' Dad called, from the other side of the room. 'Do you fancy helping me change Roz's nappy?!'

'EEEEUGH!'

Jealousy grimaced. 'What kind of a question is **THAT**?! No **WAY**!'

'Er, yeah, just coming, Dad!' called Jaz.

She picked Jel up by her pigtails and spoke firmly. 'I don't want you ruining this, Jel. I've decided I'm going to be helpful. Now, *please* go away!'

'OK, OK!' Jel shouted. 'Keep yer cool!

I was only tryin' to help. But jus' so ya know, it ain't my fault if your party sucks!' Jaz put Jel back down and she strutted off along the mantelpiece and slid down a tall lamp like a firefighter. 'HOPE YA DON'T MISS MEEEEE!'

she cackled.

'Oh, don't worry,' Jaz murmured. 'I *won't*.'

She went over to help Dad change Roz's nappy. At first, it was hard because Roz kept wriggling around like a giant worm. Jaz worried she'd get poo everywhere! At one point, she thought she could hear DJ Disaster's awful music.

But then Dad showed Jaz how to hold Roz's legs up with one hand and slip the nappy under her with the other.

Dad smiled. 'Well done, Jazmin! You're a natural!'

At bedtime, Jaz crossed off the number of days until her birthday. Then she waited for one of her parents to come in to read her a bedtime story, like they always did.

'Just coming!' shouted Dad.

'It's OK, I'll do it in five minutes!' called Mum. 'Jazzy, start reading to yourself!'

So Jaz took out a book and started to read. She tried to do Mum's funny voices but they weren't as good. There were also words she didn't understand, which made her annoyed.

She slammed the book shut and looked at her **ALIEN PET SHOP**™ clock. Five minutes had *definitely* passed. It was more like fifteen! Jaz could hear Mum singing a lullaby to Roz. Dad was on his phone telling someone all about the birth, **AGAIN**.

Jaz took the birthday-party notebook from under her pillow and started to read it, but very soon she drifted off to sleep, all by herself.

Chapter 6

The next morning at breakfast, Mum and Dad were **NOT** in a good mood. They had hardly slept all night because Roz had been feeding so much. They looked like they'd been dragged through a hedge backwards. Several times.

Roz was not much better. She had a new cry, which was very loud and fast, like a car alarm:

'WA WA WA WA WA!'

The crying was making Roz so red in the face, she looked like she was about to explode any minute. Jaz wondered what would come out of her if she did explode. Probably not lava. Possibly poo. But hopefully glitter and confetti, Jaz thought.

'Can you just hold Rosana for a second?' Mum asked Jaz.

She was trying to untie her top but Roz was wriggling too much and still crying. Jaz had just started to spread a hot piece of toast with a thick layer of Yumella chocolate spread.

'Er, hang on, I just need to do this first.'

'Jaz . . .' Mum sighed. 'That can wait.'

'Just a minute!' Jaz said, still concentrating on her own breakfast. It was very important to spread the Yumella to each corner of the toast. It was **SO** disappointing when you ate a bit without enough chocolate on it.

'Jazmin!' Dad said sharply. 'Can't you see your mum is trying to breastfeed your sister? Just hold her please. I'm doing the laundry!'

Jaz looked at her perfect piece of toast and then at her parents and then at her raspberry-red-faced sister. A hot, chocolatey piece of toast really *couldn't* wait. But Jaz pushed her plate away and held out her arms with an enormous sigh.

Mum passed Rosana to Jaz. As soon as

she did, her crying got even louder.

'Hold her closer to you!' Dad said. 'Don't be afraid.'

'Don't forget to support her head!' Mum called from the sofa.

'She's wriggling **SO** much!' Jaz moaned.

'Just relax!' Dad said. 'Then she'll stop.'

Roz did eventually stop. But not because Jaz had relaxed. It was because she was getting ready to . . .

'BLEUUUUUUUUURGH!'

Chapter 7

Jazmin could *not* believe it. She was *covered* in yucky, milky **BABY SICK**! It was on her face, dripping down her neck and all over her favourite Skater Dog dress. GROSS!

'Quick, take her off me!' Jaz yelped, holding the baby at arm's length.

Mum was still fiddling with her top. Dad

seemed to be taking FOREVER to dry
his hands.

'It's all dripping down me!' Jaz shouted.

'Calm down, Jazmin,' Dad said. 'There's
hardly anything. It's just a bit of milk.'

'A BIT OF MILK?!' Jaz said.

She stared at Dad like he was mad.

'Oh, look at your little face!' Mum cooed
at Rosana. 'You're so cute!'

Jaz could not see what was cute about
Roz right now. She was cross-eyed, pale
and stinky. White vomit was drooling
from the corner of her mouth. She looked
like a **MONSTER**.

'Eugh,' Jaz said, as Mum took the baby

from her. Dad started wiping the sick off Roz's face and clothes.

'What about ME?' Jaz moaned.

'Hang on!' Dad said impatiently.

'You're not a baby, Jaz,' Mum laughed. 'Why don't you go to the bathroom and clean yourself up?'

'Yes, you're going to be eight years old very soon!' Dad said. 'I'm sure you'll manage!'

UGH! Jaz groaned to herself as she stomped off. Mum and Dad were being SO annoying. They could write their own book of The Most Annoying Things To Say Of All Time EVER.

In the bathroom, Jaz started cleaning herself when she heard some familiar music. Suddenly, DJ Disaster appeared, swinging from the towel rail!

'DA DA DA DAAAAAA!
IT'S A PUKING
DISAAAAASTERRRRR!'

he sang.

Another voice started singing, 'They don't love you **any mooooooooore**!'

It was Jel, holding Jaz's toothbrush like it was a microphone. Jaz had to admit, Jel did have a very nice voice. And now there was Loner too, crooning along with her!

'Seriously, dude?' she said to him. 'You're friends with this one now?'

'She's **funnyyyyy**!' Loner sang, looking soppily at Jel.

'Hey!' a small voice shouted. A tiny, one-eyed, big-eared thing jumped out from behind the shower curtain. 'You said *I* could start! This is **NOT** what we planned in rehearsal, people!'

'I'm sorry, I'm sorry!' Jel said, rolling her many eyes. 'Ladies and gentlemen, please welcome **CHANGE** on to the bathroom sink! Give it up for Change!'

Jel and Loner were the only ones who clapped. Disaster was too busy checking all the electrical devices in the bathroom to see if they were dangerous. Jaz just stood in shock. She definitely wasn't expecting *another* Worry to appear. Three was quite enough.

Change took hold of the toothbrush microphone. 'What am I supposed to do with this?' she cried. 'It's a *toothbrush*!'

'Use your imagination!' Jel hissed.

Change frowned. 'I don't have one. Never mind,' she said, tossing the toothbrush to one side. 'I'll just sing *louder* instead. **NO CH-CH-CH-CH-CHANGES**!' she screeched.

Change's voice was like a sheep being strangled. It was so loud and terrible that even the bathroom mirror

CRACKED!

'Uh-oh. **DISASTER**!' said Disaster:

Chapter 8

'**OH NO!** What are we going to do?'
Jaz cried.

'I'll fix it!' Disaster shouted. He whipped
out a toolbox from goodness knows where.
'I'm always equipped for **DISASTER**!'

He started putting thick brown sticky
tape over the crack in the mirror. It looked
even worse.

'Here, allow me,' Jel said. 'I'm a genius at covering things up. Broken furniture, bad hair-cuts, bank robberies . . . you name it!'

She clambered on to the shelf above the mirror where there was a trailing plant. Then, with all her strength, she moved one of the

plants so that the leaves draped over the mirror.

'Voilà! You can't see anything now!'

'Yeah, *exactly*,' Jaz groaned.

'Everything all right in there?' came Mum's voice from outside. 'Did you get all the sick off, love?'

'Yeah, FINE!' Jaz called.

'Roz is a bit calmer now if you want a cuddle! It was just a bit of reflux.'

'I haven't a clue what reflux is,' Jel whispered to Jaz. 'But just say **NO**!'

'Maybe in a bit, Mum!' Jaz called, putting her hand over Jel's big mouth.

'OK, love, well, we'll just be in her bedroom.'

'You mean **YOUR** bedroom!' Change mumbled when Mum had gone away. 'I do **NOT** understand why you agreed to that!'

'Look, can you all just GO?' Jaz sighed. 'This is really *not* a good time.'

'I know, honeyyyyyy!' Jel sang, picking up her toothbrush microphone again. 'That's why we're heeeeeeere!'

Loner joined in. 'We're gonna help youuuuuuuu!'

'Help me?' said Jaz, doubtfully. 'How?'

'I'm gonna get your party starteeeeed!'

Jel sang again.

'OK, can you *please* stop singing?' said Jaz, scrubbing more sick off her top. 'Just . . . talk normally.'

Jel took the sponge from Jaz and started wiping her down.

'Look what she did to you! That's the problem with babies. They look cute but they're actually *animals*.'

'I agree,' said Change, folding her arms. 'Babies are **noisy**

and **messy**

and **STINKY**.

They change *everything*.'

'But it is nice having company!'
Loner shrugged.

'Hush!' Jel snapped. 'You are not
HELPING! We are on *Jazmin's* side,
remember?!'

Loner tried to protest. 'I am too, but –'

'Enough of the backchat, Loser!' Jel
interrupted.

'It's a-a-actually, er, Loner,' he stuttered.

'You need to stand up to her!' Jaz
whispered to Loner.

'I'm trying!' he whispered back,
desperately. 'She's just so . . . terrifying!'

'Look, I ain't gettin' nowhere with
you dummies.' Jel sighed. 'I'm gonna

go sort this out for myself.'

She leaped off the sink and grabbed the door handle with both hands.

'Where are you going?' Jaz said, slightly panicked.

But Jel ignored her and just kept on swinging on the handle until the door opened. Then she jumped down and marched off down the hallway.

'Uh-oh, I sense the D word coming!' Disaster shouted.

'I can't miss THIS!'

Jealousy strode majestically into the living room, with Jaz and the other three Worries huffing and puffing behind her. She jumped on to the arm of the chair that Dad was trying to snooze in.

'Hey, mister!' she shouted in his face. Dad jumped and opened his eyes.

'Who on earth are **YOU**?

JAZMIIIIIIN!' he called.

Jaz had hidden behind the door with embarrassment. She stuck her head out and opened her mouth to speak. But Jel butted in instead.

'I'm Jealousy, one of yer daughter's Worries. We need to have a little talk.'

'Well, pleased to meet you, Jealousy.' Dad frowned, sitting up. He didn't *look* pleased to meet her. Jel *was* pretty rude.

'Jazmin is very upset,' Jel continued. 'She's been cryin'. **A LOT**.'

'*Jealousy!*' Jaz hissed.

'Well, maybe if you stopped worrying her, she wouldn't be so . . . worried,' said Dad.

'Ha, ha! Very **funnyyyy**,' said Jel sarcastically. 'But you know as well as I do, it takes a lot to get rid of us Worries – *especially* a Worry as tough as Jealousy!'

'Is that right?' said Dad, folding his arms. 'So tell me, what would it take to get rid of *you*?'

'Well, I would love – I mean, *Jazmin* would love – that big birthday party you promised!'

'I don't know about a *big* birthday party,' Dad said. 'That's too much work now, with Rosana being born early.'

Change stormed forward now. 'But you **PROMISED**! You can't go back on a promise. That's **UNFORGIVEABLE**.'

'And who are you?' Dad asked.

'That's Change, but ignore her,' Jel said. 'It's ME ya need to be listenin' to. This birthday party is REAL important, ya hear? It'd better be big.'

'I'll have a think about it,' Dad said. 'But we need to go to the supermarket now.'

'To buy the party things!' Jel said. 'That's the spirit, mister!'

'Ooh, I LOVE supermarkets!' Loner shouted, jumping up and down. 'All those PEOPLE!'

'And all that *chocolate!*' Jel grinned.

'Ooh, I dunno about supermarkets,' Disaster said anxiously. 'There's almost always a pyramid of baked beans that topples over.'

'You watch too many cartoons!' Jel said, rolling her eyes and shooing the Worries towards the door. 'Let's just get outta here!'

'**Don't forget the party list!**'
Change shouted frantically. 'We *must* stick to
the list!'

'Oh no, you're not *all* coming!?' Dad
sighed as they bounced into the car.

'They'll only get up to more mischief if
they stay here,' Jaz said. 'I'll keep them under
control, I *promise.*'

Chapter 10

When they got to the supermarket, Jaz told the Worries to stay in the seat of the trolley. But pretty soon they were bouncing around and squabbling.

'Jazmin, you said you'd keep them under control,' Dad said as they arrived at the ice-cream aisle.

'I will, I will!' Jaz sighed. She moved in close to the Worries. **'SHHHHH!** If you don't stop fighting, I'll put you all in one of these freezers!'

'**Sorryyyyyy!**' they hissed
back. They were desperate to see all
the ice-cream flavours, but being shut
in a freezer would *not* be pleasant.

'I'm just going to get the nappies
and wipes,' Dad said. 'Why don't you
get some bread, Jazmin?'

'Okayyyy,' Jaz sighed. Why did
Dad never give her interesting things
to look for? Boring *bread*.
What about her party stuff!?

Jaz finally found the right aisle,
which also happened to be the
cakes and biscuits aisle.

This is more like it, she thought.

As soon as Dad was out of sight, Jel **wriggled** out of her seat, then jumped to the ground.

'We'll take this, this and this. Oh, and three of THIS!' Jel said, pulling things off the shelves and hurling them into the trolley.

'STOP!' Jaz said.

'Dad's going to go CRAZY!'

'It's for **YOUR** party!' snapped Jel. 'Don't you want it to be **AMAZING**?'

'Ooh, look at

these cupcakes – I LOVE cupcakes!' Disaster
shouted excitedly. 'They've got HEARTS all
over them!'

They did look yummy, thought Jaz.
And she *did* want to have an extra-special
birthday party.

'Come on, Jaz!' Loner said, pulling down
an extra-large packet of chocolate caramel
rolls. 'These are your favourite!'

'OK, just a few packets, then!' Jaz said, putting the cupcakes and the rolls and one or two other nice things into the trolley. She was already imagining them on a cool cake stand, offering them to all her friends.

'YEY!' the Worries whooped.

'Right! Now where is the CHOCOLATE!?' Jel shouted.

Jaz suddenly realized that Jel had got bigger. Big enough to push the trolley herself.

Chapter 11

Jaz knew she was in BIG trouble now.

'Dad! I'm SO sorry!' she shouted, running towards him. Dad was rubbing the back of his leg, surrounded by packs of nappies.

She looked around

to figure out where the Worries had gone and was so embarrassed to realize that EVERYONE in the supermarket was staring at her.

Then she spotted the Worries.

She was relieved to see they had shrunk, so no one else had seen them. Sometimes they did that for a minute, just so they wouldn't be noticed. It didn't mean that they were any less worrying, though. Jaz sometimes found this confusing.

She reached out to grab her Worries off the sweet shelves but Dad got there first.

'Right, you little rascals. Come here.'

Dad popped the Worries in the trolley, on top of the pile of cakes, biscuits and sweets. Jaz was waiting for Dad to say something about all the stuff that shouldn't be in there but he didn't seem to have noticed. He was busy pulling Rosana's baby sling out of one of the shopping bags and strapping it on.

'You four are going in here,' he said firmly. 'Right where I can see you.'

The Worries were quiet for the rest of the shopping trip and, to Jazmin's amazement, Dad didn't tell her

off for what had happened. He seemed
more worried about tracking down the No
Nonsense organic baby wipes for Roz's
bum and the right teabags for Mum.

When they got to the till, he *finally* looked
at all the stuff in the trolley: cakes, biscuits,
sweets, paper plates, cups, napkins, confetti,
funny balloons . . .

'That looks a bit . . . much.' He frowned.

UNDERSTATEMENT
OF THE YEAR,
thought Jaz.

Dad picked up a couple of things as if he was going to put them back, then sighed. 'All right, fine. Let's just get out of here. Mum will be wondering where we are.'

Jaz did a ridiculously excited dance in her head. On the way home, she kept peeking inside the shopping bags. She still couldn't believe Dad just let her get all that party stuff!

When they got home, Mum and Roz had just woken up from a nap. Jaz told Mum all about the party plans. She even had a snuggle with Roz, who seemed a lot less grumpy than before.

In fact, Jaz was so excited about all her

party stuff, she didn't even think about where the Worries were. When she remembered, she asked Dad.

'Oh, I put them in Roz's playpen as soon as we got home!' he said. 'So they wouldn't be able to get out and cause trouble!'

UH-OH. Dad didn't realize that Worries were *very* good at climbing.

When Jaz looked in Roz's room, she wasn't surprised to see that there were toys all over the place but no sign of the Worries. Jaz thought about looking for them but decided not to. She *really* needed to write the party invitations to email to all her friends! She wanted to make sure everyone could come.

'Can I do a video call with Sohal?' Jaz asked Mum.

As it was half-term, Sohal was visiting his uncle, which meant Jaz couldn't go round and see him. Mum said that she could use her phone to call his mum's phone. Jaz felt really grown up using her mum's phone. She actually knew how to use it better than Mum did.

When she'd finished talking to Sohal, Jaz felt so happy. Her head was **buzzing** with all the exciting party plans. At dinner, she couldn't stop talking about it.

At bedtime, she had another snuggle with Roz, and even told *her* all about it. She did *seem* to be listening!

Jaz didn't even mind that her parents were too busy to read her a bedtime story again. She didn't even mind Roz's crying as she fell asleep. Jaz was too busy dreaming about the

BEST BIRTHDAY PARTY EVER.

Chapter 12

It was *finally* Jaz's birthday!

And the good news was, there was still no sign of the Worries.

The first thing Jaz did was run into her parents' bedroom and give Roz a big squishy cuddle.

'Happy birthday, darling!' Mum and Dad said groggily. It looked like they'd been up all night again.

Roz blinked at Jaz and gurgled. Jaz knew this meant, 'Happy birthday too, Awesome Big Sister.'

Jaz got dressed in her party outfit, as she definitely couldn't wait until the afternoon.

Then she opened the card and presents from Mum and Dad. Normally on birthdays, they filmed her opening every single present, but Roz needed burping and it took quite a long time before she managed to let one out (but when she did it was **massive**).

Jaz was *mostly* pleased with her presents, though secretly she had expected a few more (mainly, the **ALIEN PET SHOP**™ Swervy Super Scooter). When she'd finished playing with them, she took out her birthday-party notebook and reminded Mum and Dad to sort out the jelly, the pass-the-parcel presents and various other Very Important Things.

'Don't worry, Jaz!' Mum said, pulling

out the cake ingredients with one hand and rocking Rosana with the other. 'I won't forget!'

'And, Dad, remember the music!' Jaz said.

'All under control. I've got this nifty little Bluetooth speaker linked to my phone. It's going to be brilliant. I've even borrowed a disco light from the neighbours upstairs!'

'Oh, wow!' Jaz said, feeling relieved. 'I'll start doing the decorations, then.'

It felt like **FOREVER** before the first guest arrived.

DING DONG!

It was Shara. Shara was always first to birthday parties. She had come dressed as . . . well, Jaz wasn't exactly sure.

'I'm a picnic, silly!' Shara said.

She stretched out her arms so Jaz could see the blanket she was wearing. There were lots of paper plates and pretend food stuck to it.

'I mean, I can't sit down because I'll get stabbed by a plastic fork, but it's fine.' Shara sighed.

'Cool, dude,' said Jaz.

The other guests soon arrived, all in wonderful, wacky fancy dress.

'Shall we start the party games?' Mum suggested. 'I've just put Rosana to sleep.'

'Yes, let's start with musical chairs!' Jaz said. It was her favourite.

Mum and Dad looked at one another, then around the room.

'Er, I don't think there's enough space, Jazmin.'

'**Yes, there is!**' Jaz insisted, crossing her arms.

'There really isn't,' Dad said. 'There aren't even enough chairs, even if we could fit them all in.'

'Well, you should have thought of that. I put it on my list!'

Dad gave Jaz a look which meant, *Don't be cheeky or else no TV for a week!* She unfolded her arms.

'OK, well, let's just do pass the parcel then.'

Mum went and got the parcel and Dad got the music going. 'Baa Baa Black Sheep' started playing. Everyone burst out laughing.

'That's not on the *playlist*, Dad!' Jaz groaned.

'This is kids' music, it'll do!' Dad said brightly.

'But I wrote down a list of *party* tunes. You were meant to put them on your phone!'

'Well, I didn't see that. I'm sorry, Jazmin. I'll put some cool tunes on, OK, kids?'

Dad started playing the songs he usually listened to in the bath. It was **SO** embarrassing and **NOT** cool at all.

'*Please* don't sing along,' Jaz murmured to herself, crossing all her fingers.

'AAAAAAH GAAAAAAAA DOO DOO DOO, push the mangoes, shake the tree!' Dad sang.

'OH NOOOO.' Jaz cringed. She tried to ignore him and concentrate on the parcel being thrown round the circle. Her friend Eddie kept clinging on to it, which Jaz was starting to find even more annoying than Dad's sing-a-long.

'You have to pass it on *quickly*!' Jaz said. 'Otherwise it's cheating!'

'OK, Jazmin, don't snap at your guests now!' said Mum.

Dad finally paused the music (he was enjoying the song a bit too much for Jaz's liking). It was Shara who got the parcel. Everyone held their breath and watched her unwrap the first layer.

'There's nothing in it!' Shara moaned.

'Are you sure?' Mum said, taking the paper and shaking it out. 'How strange. I must have forgotten that last one. Silly me! Take off the next layer, Shara.'

Shara ripped it off.

'There's *still* nothing!'

'Oh, I can't have forgotten *two*. Though I was feeding Rosana at the time so I might have been a bit distracted. Try again. Third time lucky!'

Something white fell out. Shara frowned. 'It looks like a . . . dirty baby wipe! **EUGH!**'

'Oh, I'm so sorry,' Mum laughed, quickly picking it up.

Jaz was soooo embarrassed. At Shara's party, there had been marshmallows with her face on them. Jaz had dirty baby wipes. It was all going wrong . . .

'Next song in three, two, one!' Dad cried. 'The "Macarena"! You'll love this one!'

The next layers were almost as embarrassing as the first three. Mum had put in a *pencil*, followed by a cough sweet, followed by a sharpener, a rubber, a bird badge and other Really Boring Things, which Jaz had definitely already seen in that messy drawer in the office. At the end, there was

ONE good thing – a pot of slime, which looked a lot like the present her parents had given her that morning . . .

Mum suggested they play musical statues next (which was definitely *not* on Jaz's list), but thankfully the doorbell rang.

DING
DOOOONG!

Maybe Mum and Dad have organized a surprise, thought Jaz. *A clown? A singer? Or maybe even . . . a magician?! This could still be the Best Birthday Party EVER!*

Chapter 13

Jaz's heart sank as she opened the door.

The Worries!

'HAPPY BIRTHDAY, JAZ!'

they all shouted at once.

They were standing on one another's
shoulders, looking absolutely ridiculous.
Jel, who was at the top, somersaulted
on to the floor.

'TA DAAAAH!'

Jel strutted in, waving like she was a
movie star. Everyone was staring at the
Worries. Jaz was SO embarrassed.

'WOW! What are they?!'

'Are they puppets?'

'ALIENS?'

'MONSTERS?!'

'They look SO cool!'

'OMG, so cuuuuute!'

'Can I stroke them?'

'Do they BITE?'

Jaz didn't know what to say. But, thankfully, Sohal did.

'They're, er, going to be doing a *show*! Later on. Come on, you guys! I'll show you to your, um, dressing room!'

Sohal took the Worries off to Jaz's bedroom and shut them in her toy cupboard. They were *not* very happy about it.

'Thanks, dude!' Jaz whispered when he came back.

'No *worries*!' Sohal winked.

'Right, time for some **DANCING**!' Dad shouted. 'The disco is all readyyyy!'

Jaz rushed over to Dad to make sure he had a better playlist than 'Nursery Time' or

'Bathtime Sing-along'. Thankfully, he had chosen some songs from *this* year.

'Right, let's hit it!' Dad said through his megaphone.

The first tune was great! Everyone was bopping **up** and **down**, shouting the words. Jaz was finally having a nice time.

And then the music suddenly stopped. Everyone stopped dancing too and stood around.

'**OH NOOO!** The speaker has run out of battery,' Dad wailed. 'But I thought I'd just charged it!'

'Use my phone,' said Mum. 'The sound is pretty good.'

The sound was actually *terrible*. No one was dancing. But Mum was sorting out the cake and Dad was too busy with Rosana to notice. Suddenly, a familiar voice blared through the megaphone.

'This is DJ Disaster IN THE HOUSE! Lemme see yer hands in the air!'

'Oh nooo,' Jaz groaned. 'How did he get out?!'

Disaster's nightmare playlist began to blast out of his speakers:

'It's a DISASTER,
'Natural DISASTER,
'Walking DISASTER.'

Not surprisingly, NO ONE was dancing.

Where's Dad? Jaz thought. *And why isn't he doing anything about it?!*

Jaz began thinking about her seventh birthday party and her sixth and her fifth.

They were all **BRILLIANT**. Her mum and dad had been so organized and fun, not distracted all the time by *Rosana*.

Just as Jaz had these thoughts, Jel shimmied on to the dance floor. She was much bigger than before. All the kids started dancing round her. She was *such* a show-off.

Next came Change, dancing really awkwardly. She kept tripping over herself and managed to make even Mum's dance moves look cool.

Loner suddenly appeared, tugging at Jaz's leg. 'When is the cake coming? **I'm hungryyyy!**'

Just then, the lights went out and Mum
came in with the cake, singing:

'HAPPY BIRTHDAY
to youuuuuuuu!'

Everyone joined in. Jaz looked around
at her friends' faces but all she could think
about were her Worries. She had no idea
what they might do or say next.

When it was time to blow out her candles,
she found she had tears in her eyes. Jaz took
off her **ALIEN PET SHOP**™ glasses and the
tears rolled down her cheeks. Jel suddenly
appeared at her side.

'Ya gotta pull yerself together, honey!' she said firmly. 'Here.' She passed Jaz a fancy handkerchief. 'Now, wipe your eyes and blow out yer candles. But don't make a wish, because that stuff's not real.'

'Hey, be quiet!' Sohal said. 'It is real, if you want it to be. Make a wish, Jaz.'

Jaz decided to listen to her friend instead of Jealousy. She blew out her candles and made her wish.

'I wish everything could go back to how it was before,' she whispered.

'**GOOD WISH!**' Change shouted, jumping up and down. 'FINALLY, *someone's* listening to me!'

Chapter 14

Sadly, nothing magical happened. The wish did not come true.

Jel was right. Jaz was still at her stupid birthday party, with her annoying Worries and her even more annoying baby sister.

'You cut the cake, Jaz!' Mum said, handing her the knife.

Anxiously, Jaz cut into the homemade

ALIEN PET SHOP™ rainbow cake. The decoration didn't look promising. Mum had tried to make Slobba Snail out of icing, but it looked more like someone had sneezed a load of purple snot on top of the cake.

The Worries didn't wait their turn for cake like everybody else. Instead, they jumped up on to the table and started helping themselves.

'**EUGH!**' Jel spluttered after shoving a whole piece into her mouth.

'It's *burnt!*'

'I think it's nice!' Sohal said sweetly.

'Cakes should be fluffy and moist! This is NOT fluffy and moist!' Change grumbled. **'EPIC FAIL!'** said Disaster, shaking his head slowly. 'It *is* pretty bad!' Loner said sadly. 'I normally love rainbow cake. But this tastes awful!'

'Don't be so rude!' said Dad. Then he tried it for himself, and had to spit it out.

'Sorry, kids,' said Mum. 'I forgot to turn the oven off when I was changing Rosana. Must've burned the bottom. The top bit's all right, though!'

Most of Jaz's friends licked the icing off and left the rest – except for Sohal, who politely finished his whole piece. The table was soon covered in slabs of burnt birthday cake.

'How could you get a birthday cake so wrong?' Change huffed. 'You just have to follow the recipe, **SILLY**!'

'Mind your manners, please!' Dad said.

'There's only one thing to do with cake this terrible!' said Jel.

Jel hurled her piece across the room and it splattered on Angus. He picked up two pieces and hurled them back. But Jel ducked, so they ended up hitting Mo and Amelia.

You can probably guess
what happened next.
If not, this is what a
food fight looks like:

Jaz put her hands over her eyes. Sohal and Loner tried desperately to stop the fight, and so did Mum and Dad. But everyone else was having far too much fun. They didn't care about the mess all over the living room.

Suddenly, Jaz got splattered in the face by Jel. Jaz was so furious she picked up an even bigger piece of cake and threw it right back at her. But Jel ducked again, so the cake landed right on . . .

ROSANA!

'Jazmin, how *could* you?!' Mum cried, scooping Roz up in her arms.

Jaz turned and ran to her bedroom, her Worries scurrying behind her, growing bigger and bigger with every step.

In her room, Jaz sat on her rug while the Worries squashed up next to her. Loner took out his guitar.

'You wanna sing?' he suggested.

'No!' Jaz snapped. She could feel so many upsetting feelings inside her, bubbling and rising like hot milk.

Just when she thought she might explode, there was a knock on her bedroom door.

Chapter 15

It was Mum and Dad. Loner was so happy to see them, he jumped up and gave them a very tight hug.

'Oh, hi, Loner,' Dad said. 'Gosh, you've . . . **grown**!'

'Hello,' Change said, shaking Mum's hand. 'I don't believe we've been introduced. I'm Change.'

'Hello, Change,' Mum said, looking the tiny creature up and down. 'Nice to meet you.'

Mum and Dad sat on the floor next to Jaz.

'Ooh, this is nice!' said Change, cuddling up to Mum. 'It's just like being a baby again! So snuggly!'

'Where's Roz?' Jaz asked.

'Asleep,' Mum said.

'And what about all my friends?'

'Don't worry. Gran has got them all

playing pin the tail on the **ALIEN PET SHOP**™ donkey. It's going down very well!'

Jaz smiled. That was a relief, at least.

'I'm really sorry about hitting Roz with the cake,' she said. 'And the mess. And, well, everything really.'

'That's all right, lovely,' Mum said, giving her a squeeze.

'Birthdays are always a little bit . . . emotional.' Dad nodded. 'Even more so when you have a new baby sister.'

'Here, we wanted to give you this,' Mum said. She handed Jaz a parcel wrapped in beautiful tissue paper and glittery ribbon. It felt very special.

'Is it a story book?' Jaz asked as she pulled it out. The cover had a lovely pattern on it but she couldn't see a title.

'Sort of,' said Dad. '*Your* story! Open it up.'

Inside, there was Mum's curly writing:

For our dearest darling Jazmin,
This photo album is to celebrate
your life so far. Look how
beautiful you are! We are so
proud of the big girl and big
sister you have grown up to be.
All our love, Mum and Dad
xxxxxxx

Jaz turned the pages and looked at the photos one by one. Some of them she'd already seen, on the computer or on Mum's and Dad's phones, but a lot of them were new. They were from when she was a tiny baby, as small as Roz, right up to now. There was something very special about seeing them like this, like she was watching herself grow.

5 days old!

11 months old

'So many CHANGES!' Change sobbed.
'I can't TAKE IT!'

'Oh, pleeeease!' Jel said, rolling her eyes.
'Enough with the waterworks!'

'Look at your parents fussing over you,'
Loner said to Jaz. 'They must've really
loved you.'

'We still DO!' Dad laughed.

'Even now *she's* here?' Jel asked, nodding her head towards the door.

'If you mean Rosana, of *course*!' Mum said. 'Love isn't something that is divided. It just gets bigger, especially when you become a big sister.'

'Are you *sure*?' Jel said, doubtfully.

'ABSOLUTELY!' Mum and Dad said at once.

Jaz got to the last page in the album. They were all photos taken in the last few days.

JAZ BECOMES A BIG SISTER! the first one said. It was her holding Roz for the first time.

The next ones had been taken without
Jaz noticing. They were of all the things
she'd done for Roz since she'd been born.
Above was written:

BEST SISTER EVER!

Disaster, who was pacing up and down in the corner, suddenly took out his DJ decks.

'**I'm BORED!** Who wants to hear some musiiiiiic?!'

'Oh no you don't!' said Dad. 'That's NOT music. Here, listen to this.'

Dad took out his phone and pressed play. It was the music Jazmin had wanted for her party.

'I finally downloaded your playlist. Sorry it's a bit late, Jazmin, but we can still enjoy it, can't we?' Dad said.

Jaz nodded.

'Come on, let's get this party started again!'

Chapter 16

Jaz followed Mum, Dad and her Worries back to the party. Thankfully, Gran and all Jaz's friends had cleaned up the mess. Dad put on Jaz's playlist and in no time everybody was dancing. Except for Disaster, of course.

'It's all very . . . *fun*.' He frowned. 'It's far too happy to dance to!'

'Just give it a minute!' Dad said. 'You'll be tapping your toes in no time!'

Sure enough, Disaster *did* start tapping his toes . . .

and dancing all over the living room . . . and all over the flat . . . and

finally out of the front door!

'**BYEEEE!** I'm off to see the world!' he shouted. 'I'm not afraid of ANYTHING! Not even pigeons pooing on my head! Bring it on, suckers!'

'Well, that was quick,' Dad said, shutting the door.

Next, it was time to open presents. Jaz received so many nice things including . . . the **ALIEN PET SHOP**™ *Swervy Super Scooter from Gran!* Even Jel admitted it was a really generous gift (and, of course, tried to steal it for herself).

Last but not least came Sohal's presents. They were both very carefully wrapped. Jaz untied the first one and found a cardboard tube made from two toilet rolls. Inside was an **ALIEN PET SHOP**™ drawing which Sohal had done himself. It was really good! The other present was a small, sparkly tin of **ALIEN PET SHOP**™ cards.

'Those are all my best cards,' Sohal said. 'The ones you don't have. I thought you'd like them.'

'I *love* them,' Jaz said, brightening. 'That is so kind, dude. Thanks.'

'You're welcome!' Sohal blushed.

The party was nearly over. Dad brought out a big box of beautiful paper bags.

THE PARTY BAGS!

Each one was full of lovely, sparkly treats, like treasure! Mum and Dad had clearly gone to a lot of trouble. Jaz handed them out to all her friends and was pleased to see how much they all loved them. She even let the

Worries have one each, as they were pretty small and quiet now. They excitedly opened their party bags and started playing with their toys straight away. The only one who wasn't impressed was Change.

'Jazmin,' she said sternly. 'These party bags do not contain **ANY** of the items on your party list! You asked for *blue bubblegum*! And *unicorn tattoos*. And *glow-in-the-dark yo-yos*. What is the point of having a list if people don't stick to it!?'

'Ah, it doesn't matter,' said Jaz. 'There are loads of other really cool things. And if you don't like it, Change, well . . . you can just give it back.'

Change stomped her foot and skulked off into the corner (but held on to her party bag).

It was time for Jaz's friends to go home now. She waved them all goodbye.

Those monsters were so AWESOME

I want those creatures at MY party!

Thanks, Jaz!

These are the best ever party bags

See ya!

SUCH a cool party, Jazmin!

Thank YOU!

BYE!

'Right, time for bath and bed!' Mum said.

'Mum, do you think I could help with Roz's bath?' asked Jaz.

'Of course, darling.' Mum smiled.

At first, Jaz found it hard to hold on to Roz as she was so slippery. But Loner helped her hold Roz's head. Then Change picked up a sponge and cleaned Roz's little body. Even Jel helped (kind of).

When bath time was finished, Jel suddenly vanished. It took Jaz a while before she spotted her again.

Once Jaz and Roz were both snug in their pyjamas, they all went into Mum and Dad's room for a bedtime story. Jaz loved being read to again. And it was better than ever with a sweet-smelling baby next to her. Even Loner fell fast asleep!

When they had finished, Jaz looked around for Change.

'Here,' Mum said, picking up something at the end of the bed. It looked like Change, but she was just a cuddly toy now. And she was actually smiling – for a change!

'You see,' said Mum, hugging Jaz close to her. 'There's no need to be afraid of change. You may be a big sister now, but you'll always be our baby.'

'Thanks, Mum,' Jaz said, hugging her back.

Then Jaz gave Roz a goodnight kiss and put her finger in Roz's hand. Roz's little fingers wrapped themselves round it. It reminded Jaz of the curly flowers in their garden, wrapping round the fence. **It felt lovely.**

As she settled into her own bed and

turned out the light, Jaz realized she didn't *really* wish everything would go back to how it was before.

Being a big sister was pretty awesome, after all.